COFFEE WITH

ISAAC NEWTON

C O F F E E   W I T H

ISAAC NEWTON

MICHAEL WHITE

FOREWORD BY BILL BRYSON

DUNCAN BAIRD PUBLISHERS

LONDON

Coffee with Isaac Newton
Michael White

Distributed in the USA and Canada by
Sterling Publishing Co., Inc.
387 Park Avenue South
New York, NY 10016-8810

This edition first published in the UK and USA in 2008 by
Duncan Baird Publishers Ltd
Sixth Floor, Castle House
75–76 Wells Street, London W1T 3QH

Managing Editors: Gill Paul and Peggy Vance
Co-ordinating Editor: James Hodgson
Editor: Philip Morgan
Assistant Editor: Kirty Topiwala
Managing Designer: Clare Thorpe

Library of Congress Cataloging-in-Publication Data Available
ISBN-10: 1-84483-611-8   ISBN-13: 978-1-84483-611-6
10 9 8 7 6 5 4 3 2 1
Printed in China

For information about custom editions, special sales, premium and corporate
purchases, please contact Sterling Special Sales Department at 800-805-5489
or specialsales@sterlingpub.com.

Publisher's note:
The interviews in this book are purely fictional, while having a solid basis in biographical
fact. They take place between a fictionalized Isaac Newton and an imaginary interviewer.

CONTENTS

Foreword by BILL BRYSON

In a basement room of the Royal Society in London, Joanna Corden, the society's friendly archivist, opens a white box and gently lifts out one of that learned institution's most venerated relics: the death mask of Isaac Newton, made on the evening of his death in 1727.

It ought to be a thrilling moment – this is, after all, the closest we can come to the physical presence of the most fertile and intriguing mind of its age – and yet, as Corden had promised, there is something oddly disappointing in Newton's impassive visage. You don't expect a death mask to be terribly expressive, of course, but this one has an almost determined blankness to it.

"Even in death," notes Corden, "he didn't give much away."

We stare respectfully at the mask for half a minute, then she returns it to the box and replaces the lid, and I realize that already I'm beginning to forget what he looked like.

Perhaps no great figure in history has been harder to know and understand than Isaac Newton. Indeed he is doubly unknowable – first because of the complexity of so much of his science and second because of the secrecy and very real oddness with which he conducted so much of his life. Here is a man who spent three decades as an academic hermit in Cambridge, as withdrawn from worldly affairs as one could be, but then in late middle age became a fêted public figure and comparative gadfly in London. He could unpick the most fundamental secrets of the universe, yet was equally devoted to alchemy and wild religious surmise. He was prepared to invest years in embittered fights over credit for the priority for discoveries, yet cared so little for conventional adulation that his most extraordinary findings were sometimes kept locked away for decades. Here is, in short, a man who was almost wilfully unknowable.

Corden brings out another of the Society's treasures – a small reflecting telescope made by Newton himself in 1669. It is only six inches long but exquisitely made. Newton ground the glass himself, designed the swivelling socket, turned the wood with his own hand. In its time this was an absolute technological marvel, but it is also a thing of lustrous beauty. The man who made this instrument had sensitivity and soul as well as scientific genius.

"It's strange, isn't it," says Corden, reading my thoughts, "that you can feel more in his presence from one of his instruments than from his own death mask."

There really never was a more private man. So how lucky we are to have this volume in which Michael White deftly brings this impossible character to life, and makes his frequent wild actions and wayward notions seem almost reasonable. Even better, White conveys to us Newton's most challenging scientific concepts in terms that render them logical and wondrously, instantly comprehensible, and in so doing he fully captures the excitement, satisfaction and very real beauty of scientific discovery.

So prepare yourself for an unusual treat. You are about to enter one of the greatest minds in history.

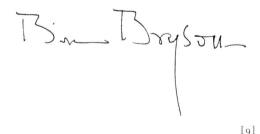

INTRODUCTION

Isaac Newton was a man who transcended the age in which he lived, and in terms of his influence on the modern world, he is without peer. He formulated the theory of gravity, devised a radically new theory of light and created a calculus that would revolutionize mathematics. His most famous work, *Principia Mathematica*, is arguably the most important scientific book ever published: it explains his theory of matter in motion, which, a generation after his death, sparked the Industrial Revolution.

Newton achieved a phenomenal amount in one lifetime, and he really had several careers. He was a scientist and a mathematician who later became an administrator, serving first as a Member of Parliament, then as Master of the Royal Mint. Late in life, he turned the Royal Society from a dilettante's club into an eminent scientific organization. Although he was extremely pious and a devout Christian, he was thoroughly unorthodox in his religious beliefs and spent much time exploring aspects of arcane knowledge, including the taboo subject of the occult.

The premise of this book is a conversation between myself and Isaac Newton. The setting is left to the imagination of the reader, but we may assume that the interview takes place at the very end of Newton's life when he is able to reflect on his achievements and the key events of his time.

Newton was a disagreeable man who was often unpleasant and antisocial; consequently, he had few friends. He relied entirely upon his own counsel and one had to work hard to earn his respect. He might have been resistant to a conversation such as the one here, but equally, he liked others to know of his brilliance, a commodity he possessed in abundance.

ISAAC NEWTON (1642–1727)
His Life in Short

The iconic image of Isaac Newton is that of a young
man in 17th-century attire, musing on the nature
of the universe while sitting under the hanging
branches of a tree. Serendipitously, an apple falls on
his head, and in this inspired moment his thoughts
gel and his genius releases a flood of ideas that bring
forth the theory of universal gravitation and, with it,
a law to explain the action of gravity.

This is a romantic notion, and one probably
based only vaguely on the truth. Certainly there were
apple trees in the garden of his mother's home in
Woolsthorpe (the house in which he was born). Those
trees are still there and it is likely Isaac Newton did
indeed sit under them from time to time. He visited
his mother during the summer of 1665, fleeing

Cambridge as plague spread beyond London. And this was also the summer in which he began to get somewhere with his thinking about gravitation. But the idea that Newton saw the whole complex array of his theory in the very moment the apple was supposed to have fallen is overly simplistic and almost certainly a glamorous invention, one probably contrived by Newton himself to obfuscate the real story.

———

Isaac Newton was born on Christmas Day 1642 into a relatively prosperous family from the village of Woolsthorpe in Lincolnshire. His father, also named Isaac, was an illiterate farmer and landowner who married Hannah Ayscough, a local girl from a socially superior family which had recently lost most of its lands and capital through a series of bad investments.

At this time, England was in the grip of the Civil War. That summer, the earliest skirmishes in the conflict between rival political and religious groups had begun to escalate into a savage bloodletting in which families were torn apart over ideological differences, and often brothers found themselves on opposing sides. On a superficial level, the Civil War was a clash between those who supported the monarchy (the Cavaliers) and those who wanted to depose King Charles I (the Roundheads); but it was also a war between Catholics and Protestants, a conflict that had its roots in the schism with Rome precipitated by Henry VIII almost a century earlier. Newton's family were staunchly Protestant and Charles I was strongly pro-Catholic, so it is most likely the family would have supported the Roundhead cause in the war.

Isaac Newton's father died before his son was born, and the baby, who arrived two months premature, was said to have been so small he could fit into a quart pot. Indeed, he was not expected to live long. When the boy was three years old, his mother, Hannah, remarried. Her new husband was Reverend Barnabas Smith, a local vicar who did not want Isaac living with them. So the child was brought up by his grandparents at the family home in Woolsthorpe.

This event traumatized Newton and acted as a powerful force in shaping his character. He loathed his stepfather and wrote in his diary that he wanted to kill the man. Throughout his schooldays he remained detached and introverted. He did not do particularly well at school until about the age of fourteen when he was noticed by his headmaster, Henry Stokes, who encouraged him and boosted his confidence.

While he was at the King's School in Grantham, Newton lived for a while with a family called the Clarks, who ran an apothecary. Mr Clark's brother, Dr Joseph Clark, had been a successful academic at

Cambridge University but had died young, leaving behind an impressive library of arcane texts which were stored in a backroom behind the shop. The collection included radical books by Galileo, Giordano Bruno and René Descartes, and Newton worked his way through the entire library before being accepted into Trinity College, Cambridge, in 1661.

Soon after going up to Cambridge, Newton came under the influence of older scholars who saw something in him and encouraged him. Most important among these were the Cambridge Fellows Humphrey Babington, Henry More and Isaac Barrow.

From 1664 Newton conducted experiments to discover the true nature and character of light. He based his early ideas on those of Descartes but soon outstripped him in analyzing the way light behaved under different conditions. He formulated mathematical descriptions of reflection, refraction and diffusion, explained the nature of colour and demonstrated how a spectrum could be formed and manipulated. He recorded his findings but kept them to himself because, even then as a young student, he was suspicious of the intentions of others and was paranoid that his ideas might be stolen if he attempted to publish anything.

The year between the summers of 1665 and 1666 has been called Newton's *annus mirabilis*, and with good reason. During this astonishing twelve-month period he laid the mathematical foundations for his theory of gravity and articulated his three laws of motion, which formed the basis of the new scientific discipline of mechanics. He also developed further his ideas about optical phenomena, began building his first telescopes and devised his calculus and another important mathematical tool called the binomial theorem.

Isaac Newton was made a Fellow of Trinity College in 1668, succeeding his mentor Isaac Barrow to become the second Lucasian Professor of Mathematics at Cambridge (the seat held more than 300 years later by Stephen Hawking). He was only 27, the youngest man ever to hold the chair. By the time he was 30 he had become a Fellow of the Royal Society.

The seeds of Newton's greatest contributions to science were planted early in his career, but these really were only seeds. His theory of universal gravitation was a strikingly original concept to explain one of the great forces at work in the universe, the force that keeps the planets in their orbits and the stars and galaxies in their courses. It did not come to him in one miraculous moment, but took almost twenty years to evolve and was the result of many influences, especially mathematics and alchemy, countless scientific experiments he conducted in his rooms and a multitude of observations he had made of planets and comets using his telescope. The theory did not fully take shape until he wrote his great book, *Principia Mathematica*, which he began in 1684 and saw published in 1687. Today, this is regarded as probably the most influential scientific treatise ever written.

The first major influence on the theory of universal gravitation was mathematics. Isaac Newton was a supreme mathematician, who was, by the age of 24, the most advanced of his time. He was also a versatile natural philosopher, and long before he was made a professor he had absorbed the entire canon of science up to his time. By the plague year of 1665, he had studied in detail the work of all the major mathematicians of the era, including John Wallis, Robert Boyle and René Descartes, and had made his own original contributions. For example, he took Descartes's concept of Cartesian coordinates (the graphical representation of points between axes x, y and z), which the Frenchman described in his *Discourse on Method* (1637), and produced a mathematical interpretation of Galileo's ideas of acceleration. He also illustrated how his own calculus could be used to solve practical problems.

Around the same time, Newton devised a generalized version of an algebraic technique called the binomial theorem, which allows mathematicians to calculate the power of sums (the value of any two numbers x and y added together and taken to any power n). It is believed that a limited form of the theorem (for small values of n such as squares and cubes) was known to the Indian mathematician Pingala during the 3rd century BC, but Newton was the first to create a general theorem for *any* value of n.

Using his mathematical talents he began to understand that gravity was responsible for keeping the planets in motion and suggested a mathematical relationship linking the distance between two bodies (such as planets) and the force of gravity between them – a relationship he called the inverse square law. This was a great accomplishment, but neither Newton nor anyone else at the time could understand how this force actually operated.

The second influence to guide Newton along the road to his theory of universal gravitation was alchemy and the occult tradition. During the 17th century, the idea that an object could influence the movement of another without actually touching it was unimaginable. Such behaviour is now called "action-at-a-distance" and we take it for granted, but in Newton's day it was seen as magical, an occult property. But thanks to his experiments in alchemy,

Newton could approach gravity with a more open mind than most of his peers.

Newton was never interested in studying alchemy for personal gain or for making gold. His sole purpose was to find what he believed were hidden basic laws that governed the universe. He was a Puritan who believed in the idea of God's "Word" and God's "Works". He was devoted to the teachings of the Bible – God's "Word" – and he believed that it was his duty to unravel the puzzle of life, to investigate everything there was to know about the world; in other words, to study God's "Works".

During Newton's lifetime, alchemy was a crime, punishable by death. Not only that, but any hint that he was experimenting with alchemy would have destroyed his academic reputation. But this belies the fact that Newton actually spent far more time on alchemical research than he did on orthodox scientific practice. When he died in 1727, Newton was discovered to have owned the largest library of occult literature ever collected; he had himself written more than a million words on the subject, along with at least a million more words analyzing the Old Testament and interpretations of the prophets.

Newton began investigating alchemy in 1669. He travelled to London to buy forbidden books from fellow alchemists and carried out his secret experiments far from the prying eyes of the authorities and his rivals within the scientific community. His earliest experiments were very basic, but after reading everything he could about the art, he soon pushed alchemy further than any of his predecessors. Unlike them, he approached experiments logically and with great precision, meticulously writing up what he had discovered.

Newton's breakthrough in alchemy came when he observed materials in his crucible and realized that they were acting under the influence of forces. He could see that some particles were attracted to each other while others were repelled by their neighbours without there being any physical contact or tangible link between them. In other words, he observed action-at-a-distance within the alchemist's crucible. He then began to realize that this might also be how gravity worked, that what he saw happening in the microcosm of the crucible and the alchemist's fire could perhaps also happen in the macrocosm – the world of planets and suns.

But there were other occult influences at work. From the mid-1670s, when he was in his early thirties, until the day he died in 1727, Newton was obsessed with religion and spent years studying comparative theology. He believed that the Hermetic philosophers of pre-Christian civilizations possessed a wealth of secret knowledge, which, if interpreted by modern thinkers, could offer clues to explain the most fundamental mechanisms of the universe. He spent many years studying original sources of biblical accounts as well as the works of earlier magi who had been inspired by the Hermetic tradition.

Newton was a difficult man, who according to contemporaries had very little sense of humour. According to one story, a student who was taught by the Lucasian professor for 18 months saw him laugh only once – when the boy asked him what possible use could be made of Euclid's mathematics. He was taciturn and relished his own company. From 1661 until he left Cambridge and academia in 1696, he lived the life of a recluse, rarely engaging in college activities and leaving his laboratory only when necessary.

For more than twenty years, Newton shared rooms with a theologian named John Wickins whom he had met soon after going up to university. Wickins may have acted as Newton's amanuensis, at least in the early days of their relationship. For the historian and the biographer, he is a frustratingly enigmatic character. He was probably the person who knew Newton the best, but sadly, he left almost no record of their years together and nothing at all concerning their personal relationship. In 1683 Wickins left Cambridge to accept an appointment as a clergyman in a village near Monmouth. It appears that there may have been an acrimonious split, because the two men never spoke to each other again. Mystery surrounds the reason for this fracture and for Wickins's rather sudden departure.

Newton clashed at one time or another with almost all of his contemporaries, and there were few he could have called "friends". Many people were acquainted with Newton and appreciated his amazing talents, but no one really knew him. He was secretive and quick to anger, and he guarded jealously his position as one of the most important scientists of the age.

Soon after becoming a Fellow of the Royal Society, Newton clashed with Robert Hooke (1635–1703), who was then the Curator of Experiments at the Society. He had an even more bitter and longer-lasting feud with another great mathematician of his generation, Gottfried Leibniz (1646–1716), a man sometimes referred to as the "German Newton". Both men had independently created a system of calculus, but Newton believed that the younger Leibniz had stolen the idea from him. It is perhaps telling that the mathematical notation Newton developed for calculus was rather cumbersome and far less user-friendly than Leibniz's. There is evidence to show that Newton actually made no attempt to make his method easy to understand and use. He often referred to those he perceived as amateur mathematicians as "smatterers" who should not try to understand the intricacies of the subject. It is probable that he made his version of the calculus deliberately exclusive.

In 1693 Newton experienced a nervous breakdown. Evidence for this comes from a collection of very odd letters he wrote to colleagues and comments he made to associates. The cause of this short-lived mental illness has never been determined for sure. It has been suggested that he became ill through ingesting too much mercury during his alchemical experiments, or that he simply placed too much of a burden on himself and suffered mental and physical exhaustion.

Another possibility is that by 1693 he perceived a great flaw in his alchemical explorations. These had been crucial in his elucidation of the theory of universal gravitation, but he had always yearned to discover a theory to describe forces that operated on the atomic scale—a companion theory to his explanation of gravitation. It may finally have dawned on him that he would never achieve his goal of obtaining the Philosopher's Stone which he believed was essential to an understanding of the structure of the microcosm in the same way that his law of universal gravitation described one of the key aspects of the macrocosmic world.

Soon after his breakdown, Newton abandoned experimental science altogether. He left Cambridge and became first the Warden, then the Master, of the Royal Mint at the Tower of London. This marked the beginning of an entirely new phase in his life. He remained a private man, but he also started to become something of a social climber and ingratiated himself with the most powerful figures in the country, including the Royal Family. He made a great deal of money from shrewd and sometimes lucky financial dealings and became one of the most respected and powerful figures within the Establishment of the early 18th century. He was knighted by Queen Anne in 1705.

At the Royal Mint, Newton was merciless toward any criminals who tried to steal from the state. He persecuted with obsessive zeal "clippers" (men and women who clipped pieces of gold and silver from coins), and he is said to have attended every hanging of a clipper during his time as Master of the Royal Mint, even though it was not a requirement of his job.

After leaving Cambridge, Newton never returned to alchemy nor to any form of experiment, although his expert scientific opinion was sought by many and he presided over the Royal Society for more than 23 years from 1703 until his death in 1727. In his later years he split his time between administrative duties at the Mint, his role as President of the Royal Society and his very active participation in the whirlwind of London high society. He established friendly relations with many important figures of the day, including Jonathan Swift, Christopher Wren and Edmund Halley.

Isaac Newton saw eight different monarchs on the throne of England; he lived through the Commonwealth and bore witness to the Glorious Revolution of 1688, after which he served briefly as a Member of Parliament for Cambridge University. When he died, he was given a state funeral and buried in Westminster Abbey, where an elaborate tomb bears a Latin inscription, which translates as:

Here lies Isaac Newton, Knight, who by a strength of mind almost divine, and mathematical principles peculiarly his own, explored the course and movements of the planets, the paths of comets, the tides of the sea, the dissimilarities in rays of light and, what no other scholar has previously imagined, the properties of the colours thus produced. Diligent, sagacious and faithful in his expositions of nature, antiquity and the Holy Scriptures, he vindicated by his philosophy the majesty of God Almighty, and expressed the simplicity of the Gospel in his manners. Mortals rejoice that there has existed such and so great an ornament of the human race! He was born on December 25th, 1642 and died on March 20th, 1727.

On the tomb sits a huge marble statue of Newton, and at his feet cherubs play. He leans regally on a pile of four books entitled: "Divinity", "Chronology",

"Optica" and "Phil Princ. Math". A similar tome
entitled "Alchemy" is conspicuous by its absence.

————

Not everyone has appreciated the great work that
Isaac Newton produced. He was disliked by a
generation of Romantics in the early 19th century,
who saw his legacy as a brutish thing, and believed
that, somehow, the knowledge Newton provided
destroyed the mystique and majesty of the human
perception of Nature. William Blake and Lord Byron
were particularly anti-Newtonian in their outlook.

Yet it is impossible to overestimate the
contribution to human advancement made by Isaac
Newton. Einstein said of him: "His clear and wide-
ranging ideas will retain their unique significance
for all time as the foundation of our whole modern
conceptual structure in the sphere of natural
philosophy." But beyond even this, Newton's work is

the very cornerstone of modern technology: his work gave substance to the Enlightenment, and a little later, the Industrial Revolution. Without his three laws of motion, the dawn of the technological age would have been delayed considerably and all our lives would be very different.

Although Einstein refined the ideas of Newton, his special and general theories of relativity are only important in extreme situations, such as when we consider the behaviour of matter travelling at close to the speed of light. For almost all everyday purposes, Newton's laws created in the 17th century serve us perfectly well, and his theories are as relevant to our lives today as they have ever been. It is a sobering thought that the mathematics used by space engineers to guide spacecraft to the Moon and beyond is entirely Newtonian.

NOW LET'S START TALKING …

Over the following pages, Isaac Newton engages in an imaginary conversation covering fourteen themes, responding freely to searching questions.

The questions are in red italic type;
Newton's answers are in black type.

THE WOUNDS OF CHILDHOOD

Newton never knew his father, and when he was
three years old his mother Hannah remarried.
For some unknown reason his stepfather, the
Reverend Barnabas Smith, did not want his new
wife to have any further contact with Isaac. As a
result, she was moved to a neighbouring village
but did occasionally visit her son while the boy
was being raised by his ageing grandparents.
This disruptive experience almost certainly
damaged Isaac Newton and was influential in
making him the person he was.

*Good morning, Sir Isaac, thank you for agreeing to
this conversation. There are so many aspects to your
extraordinary life, I hardly know where to begin. But
perhaps a good place to start might be to ask what it was
that made you so combative with your contemporaries?*

I like the word "combative", young man. I am just
that, and I don't consider it a fault.

*I wasn't implying it was a fault as such, Sir Isaac. But
I can't help wondering what the root of this could be.
Forgive me if you feel I'm being too personal, but it's well
known that you went through a childhood trauma when
your mother remarried. Do you think this may have had
a dramatic effect on the moulding of your character?*

It is indeed a very personal question, and I find it
very difficult to talk of such things, but then I have

nothing to hide. My life story is well documented, and as you say, my mother did leave me to grow up with my grandparents. They were very kind to me and gave me their love. And I did still see my mother from time to time. I never blamed her – she did the logical thing by remarrying. What woman in her position could refuse? But I admit I did detest my stepfather, the Reverend Barnabas Smith.

And do you think this trauma in your childhood influenced your character? For example, you never married. Did you ever contemplate family life?

No, to be honest, I never did. My mind has been filled with other things. I don't believe there would have been room in my life for a family, for marriage. I'm very fond of my niece Catherine and she lived with me in London for a time before she married and had a family of her own. There was a girl I liked very much in Woolsthorpe, Catherine Storer, but that relationship came to nothing. I went to Cambridge and soon I was "married" to learning.

Do you have any regrets about that?

Not at all. If I had the chance to change the past, I would alter nothing. The pursuit of knowledge has fulfilled me entirely. Besides, I followed my calling. I don't believe I had any choice in the matter.

And you did eventually enjoy a more regular relationship with your mother, didn't you?

Reverend Smith died in 1653 when I was eleven. My mother had three children by the man and then returned with them to the house in Woolsthorpe. I imagine she hoped we would just continue where we had left off, but it was very difficult for me. I did, though, eventually warm to my three half-siblings, and my mother and I forged new bonds. However, my mother was never supportive of my interest in learning. She wanted me to take on the running of our small estate in Woolsthorpe and she did not appreciate the value of education. This created bad feeling between us and I went through a rebellious phase. My mother insisted I leave school and work on the land. Instead, I paid a farm hand to do my chores for me while I escaped to read.

And later, when you were at university, you maintained a close relationship with your family?

To an extent. I travelled home to Woolsthorpe when I could. I spent some months there in 1665 during the worst of the plague – Lincolnshire was something of a safe haven, far from the cities where the disease was most rampant. And then, in May 1679, I spent several weeks nursing my mother on her death bed. She had been prescribed some quack medicine by the local doctor. I formulated another treatment, but she died in early June that year. We talked long into the night during her last days, just the two of us alone in the house. We resolved any remaining differences and we made our peace with each other.

INSPIRATIONS

Isaac Newton was born the year Galileo died,
and to many historians of science he is seen
as the Italian's natural heir. Indeed, while
exceptionally brilliant people like Newton
and Galileo have appeared at different points
in history and have precipitated massive
shifts in human understanding, they all
found inspiration and guidance from their
predecessors. Newton was, of course, no
exception to this rule, for he built his own
models upon a rich heritage of philosophical
reasoning – from the work of Archimedes and
Aristotle to Copernicus, Kepler and Galileo
himself.

So, just to put your work into perspective, where was scientific knowledge around the time you entered Cambridge?

That's a very difficult question to answer, but in summary it's as follows: Galileo had shown that the Earth was not the centre of the universe, but orbited the Sun just like any other planet. Kepler had shown that these orbits were elliptical. Six planets were observable, along with the satellites of Jupiter. Craters had been observed on the Moon. Many of Galileo's discoveries had dispensed with the ideas of Aristotle, which had percolated down to us as accepted wisdom for two millennia. Galileo had shown there was a force acting on falling objects which drew them to the Earth at a certain speed, but even he had no notion of a law to describe this observation. So I was born into an age ripe for discovery, and with the good fortune to have the foundations laid by some remarkable men who preceded me.

Actually, that's what I was going to ask you next. Who are the thinkers of the past who've most inspired you?

There have been many great minds who have each contributed a piece here and a piece there. Human knowledge is like an endless road: one outstanding person lays a stretch of the road, another the next section. Each road builder lays stretches of different sizes.

But who would you say are the most inspiring of the masters?

If I were forced to offer an opinion on this, I should have to place Archimedes at the pinnacle of human achievement in pure mathematics and natural philosophy. I would name Galileo Galilei as the most brilliant of recent times.

Why Archimedes?

Archimedes was a unique talent. So much is made of Aristotle and his so-called great contributions, but Archimedes outstrips him in every way. Archimedes had an innate, natural, effortless understanding of the way the universe operates, and most crucially, he could interpret this method of operation in the form of pure mathematics. He was like a cipher between God and Man. He could take an observation, such as the way water rises in a tank when an object is immersed in it, and from this create a mathematical law. He created a form of calculus (what he called "the method of exhaustion") some two thousand years before I was born and he applied it to a range of problems. I can claim to have produced a much more versatile version of this and to have put the concept into a modern mathematical idiom, but Archimedes was the first to even imagine that such a thing as calculus was possible. Archimedes also calculated an accurate approximation to *pi*. He created a method of determining accurate values for square roots of large integers and an original system for expressing large numbers. He was probably most famous for what has become known as Archimedes' Principle, a theorem that allows us to calculate the weight of any body that is immersed in a liquid.

Do you identify with Archimedes in some ways?

Actually, I like to think of myself as unique – I don't really understand the concept of identifying myself with another human being. However, if you're wondering if I see any comparisons between myself and Archimedes, there are two obvious points of connection. First, Archimedes was multi-talented in that he had a deep appreciation of theory, but he was also a practical man: he was not only a great mathematician, he devised machines to lift heavy weights, he built accurate balances and he even won a prize in Syracuse for a war machine that he'd invented. I too have the ability to work on a practical as well as a theoretical level. Second, Archimedes would often lose himself in his own world of pure intellect. It is said that he met his death at the hands of a soldier from an army invading his homeland. Apparently he was lost in thought, writing geometric shapes in the sand. The soldier had asked him to stop what he was doing and Archimedes had either not heard him or decided to ignore him. I also travel into this almost dreamlike state in which the outside world fades and dissolves, and the single focus of my mind is the thing I'm studying.

And Galileo?

Well, everything we think about Galileo is, of course, overshadowed by his trial before the Roman Inquisition. You understand that I abhor the Catholic Church and consider the Pope to be the Antichrist, but also as an empirical philosopher I am greatly angered by the destructiveness of the Vatican. If we look at Galileo's body of work objectively, it is clear that he was far ahead of his time and offered the world an enormous amount.

Such as?

Do you really not know? Well, to begin with, he is the father of experimental science. He was the first to create a scientific system – the idea that a scientist should make an observation, then formulate a mathematical model to explain it and finally create a general rule that can be applied to a range of observations closely related to the first one. So, for example, he worked out that the speed of a pendulum swing is independent of the length of the arc. He also found that the mass of the bob did not affect the speed of the pendulum at all, but that, crucially, the period of the oscillation *did* depend on the length of the string. From this, he formulated a mathematical equation which could then be applied to any situation in which a pendulum moves. Beyond this, Galileo was a great polymath. He produced a telescope that was excellent for his time and he studied the Moon and the planets with it. He showed clearly that

Copernicus had been correct to declare that the Earth orbits the Sun, not vice versa. He explained how objects experience acceleration when they fall from a higher point to a lower point. He demonstrated how cannonballs fly through a parabolic trajectory. In short, he demolished many of the archaic precepts of Aristotle.

Yes, I was going to ask you to say more about Aristotle. You mentioned earlier that Archimedes outstripped him, but you alluded to the fact that posterity has honoured Aristotle far too much and not given Archimedes his due.

I think that is correct. Aristotle is revered as the father of science, or natural philosophy. His ideas have been taught as irrefutable truth for two millennia, but he was wrong about almost everything. He believed that all matter was made of four fundamental elements: fire, earth, air and water. This is clearly a ridiculous over-simplification. He believed an object moved through the air because, as it travelled onward, it displaced air which then flowed behind the object to propel it forward! He believed we see things because particles fired out from our eyes bounce off objects and return to the eye! The man never once conducted a single experiment: he simply deduced his ideas using logic. He thought deeply about things, that cannot be denied, but his conclusions were almost always wrong, and if he had been able to bring himself to test his hypotheses he would have seen the error of his ways. Archimedes avoided this fatal flaw because he worked with both pure mathematical reasoning and a practical ability that came naturally to him.

INITIATION

Newton's education was financed anonymously
by Humphrey Babington, a gentleman-scholar
and Fellow of Trinity College, Cambridge,
who had taken the teenager under his wing.
Newton never knew that Babington was his
benefactor and assumed that the fees were paid
from his mother's estate. Once at university,
Newton was freed from any diversions or
family responsibilities and he came under
the influence of some of the best intellects of
the time, men who not only offered their own
experience but introduced him to some of the
latest ideas of science and philosophy.

I believe that you weren't overly impressed with the University of Cambridge when you first arrived there. Is that true?

It certainly is. I entered Trinity College as a "subsizar", graduating to a "sizar" after matriculation a month later. Subsizars and sizars were the poorest students at the university, and I was treated little better than a servant. I had to wait on one of the Fellows, emptying his bed pan and serving his food. Meanwhile, the majority of students came from wealthy families and they were lazy good-for-nothings who had few brains between them and were only at the university because their fathers had insisted upon it.

But ultimately you found the university intellectually satisfying?

Yes, of course. I was lucky to be accepted early on by two very important members of the university. When I was seventeen I was at school in Grantham and I lodged with an apothecary in the town. He had a wonderful collection of books which he had inherited from his deceased brother, Dr Joseph Clark. So, even before going up to Cambridge I had been introduced to all the great thinkers of the past: Aristotle, Plato and many of the occultists, mystics and alchemists of past centuries. I was also introduced to the heretical works of men such as Giordano Bruno, Copernicus and, most importantly, the great master, Galileo, whose books were then still on the Vatican's *Index Librorum Prohibitorum*, the Index of Prohibited Texts. However, as a young man, the most profound influence on me was my tutor at Trinity, Isaac Barrow, who was the Lucasian Professor before me. He had a splendid library of occult literature and had himself conducted some researches in natural philosophy. He also knew many of the most important philosophers and men of science of his time. He was involved in the establishment of the Royal Society in the early 1660s. He introduced me to the notion that no form of knowledge should be considered forbidden and that the Lord's plan may be found in all learning. Another man who was very important to my early education was a Fellow of Trinity named Humphrey Babington who came from Grantham and was related to the Clarks. Isaac Barrow and Humphrey Babington were friends, and they both helped me enormously. They gave me a superb grounding in the world of the arcane and the intellect.

Were Babington or Barrow interested in what might be called "exotic knowledge" — the Hermetic tradition and so forth?

Barrow was a very good mathematician and possessed a sharp intellect. He was a deeply religious man. Indeed, he later became Chaplain to King Charles II. He was never a practising alchemist, if that's what you really mean, but he did have some exotic titles in his library. I believe Babington was more inclined to dabble in mysticism. Neither man was afraid to read and collect works that many Establishment figures would have considered "dangerous".

Such as?

Both libraries contained radical interpretations of Copernicus, including at least one volume by the arch-heretic Giordano Bruno, along with one or two commentaries on ancient Egyptian occult knowledge.

And so, would you say that Babington and Barrow were

influential in leading you to study arcane subjects and later to begin alchemical experiments?

They were an influence, yes. Neither man spoke openly about subjects that society would proscribe as anti-orthodox or against traditional theology. And both men had taken holy orders, because it was a condition of their Fellowship. But without doubt, both men cherished the intellectual world and were liberal in their thinking about new, sometimes unconventional philosophies, and they influenced me to think more laterally and to be as open-minded as possible.

BITTER FEUDS

Newton was an egotistical man who considered himself far superior to any other intellectual of his age. He was utterly convinced that he had been chosen by God to possess the most brilliant mind of any mortal and to be nothing less than God's mouthpiece, a man who was leading humanity to a clearer understanding of the way the universe works. This, along with his dislike for most human beings, his suspicious nature and his aggressive determination to be first to achieve anything, led him into a succession of dramatic conflicts with his contemporaries.

Sir Isaac, you gained a reputation for engaging in disputes with other scientists and mathematicians. Do you think these clashes had a common cause, and if so, would you care to speculate on it?

Yes, of course there was a common cause for all the disputes in my career: I was right and the imbeciles I was up against were wrong! Need I say more?

But do you really think that's true? After all, Robert Hooke was a great experimenter. Gottfried Leibniz was a world-class mathematician. And John Flamsteed, the Astronomer Royal, with whom you also had a bitter feud, was a very capable astronomer.

You think so, do you? Well, I dare say each of these men had some qualities, but ultimately, in each battle, I was shown to be right and they were wrong.

Let us consider them in turn. Robert Hooke — there, I can barely speak the name without retching. He was a well-known experimenter, but he misunderstood my work entirely. He was Curator of Experiments at the Royal Society when I submitted my first set of optical researches, but you know, he did not even bother to read my paper properly before dismissing it out of hand. That was the start of my feud with Hooke. It was not I who began the battle, but I certainly finished it.

But didn't Hooke apologize for spending too little time on your paper, and didn't he then try to make amends?

He offered an official apology, yes, but he never liked me after that and I never, ever trusted him.

And for many years after this you rarely attended meetings of the Royal Society.

That's correct.

Is it true that your famous quote, "If I have achieved anything it is by standing on the shoulders of giants," was a direct slur on Hooke, who was a dwarf?

Well, I have no reason to deny it. I did write this in a letter to Hooke and I did mean it to cut deep. The man was a vile braggart. He never produced one worthwhile piece of original work and he constantly boasted about what he could do, without ever doing anything. A perfect example is Hooke's claims about the law of universal gravitation. In early 1684 he told Christopher Wren and Edmund Halley – my associates at the Royal Society – that he had devised a law to describe the behaviour of bodies under the influence of gravity. Wren and Halley wanted to see what I had written on the subject but Hooke persuaded them to wait and to give him a chance first. Two months passed and Hooke could come up with nothing. Finally, after another long wait, Wren and Halley grew impatient and Halley came to see me in Cambridge. I showed him what I had written on the subject, a treatise which later grew into my *Principia*. It turned out Hooke had absolutely no clue about a law of gravity and was just boasting. I find it hard to respect such individuals. Then he tried to damage me. I cannot tolerate such people.

And what of Gottfried Leibniz? Your feud with him lasted 40 years and you so hated the man that you continued to slander him in your private papers even after he'd died.

Again, I have no reason to deny these things. Leibniz was a thief, pure and simple. He stole calculus from me and tried to make out he had come up with it first.

Are you sure? Was it not perhaps a case of each of you independently coming up with the same concept?

No, it was not. I was the first to devise calculus. Leibniz stole the concept when he visited London in 1673. I had a rough draft of the idea, which I had entrusted to the publisher John Collins. He was either hoodwinked into showing this material to Leibniz or he colluded with the German.

That's surely speculation? There's no proof that Leibniz saw your draft.

You believe what you like, young man. I know what *I* believe. Calculus could only have been offered to this world through the mind of one mortal. That mortal is me. God does not waste his energies passing on such treasures to more than one man – what would be the point of that? No, Leibniz stole my calculus and he will rot in hell because of it.

There was a third great feud wasn't there? The protracted arguments you had with John Flamsteed? Could you tell me how these came about?

Yes, I'd be glad to. In 1694 I was completing the second edition of my *Principia* when I approached Flamsteed for some astronomical data. He was, of course, the Astronomer Royal and Master of the Greenwich Observatory. First, he was tardy with his responses, then he deliberately gave me very inferior information. When I challenged him over this, he became obstructive. I was forced in the end to call upon the Queen's husband, Prince George, to intercede. It was regrettable, but I can assure you the blame lay squarely with the Astronomer Royal.

A FAITH APART

Isaac Newton was a deeply religious man. Raised
as an orthodox and strict Protestant, by the
time he was in his early twenties he had left
the conventional path of his faith and become
an Arian. Subscribers to this belief refused to
accept the idea of the Holy Trinity as prescribed
by orthodoxy and claimed that Christ was
created by God rather than being an aspect
of the Holy Trinity. In 17th-century England
Arianism was considered a dissenting branch of
Christianity and was outlawed. And so, as with
many aspects of his life, Newton had to keep his
faith secret.

When did you adopt Arianism and what led you to it?

I first became interested in the early Church around 1668, and I was particularly fascinated by the notion of the Holy Trinity. I studied not only the Bible, but also the writings of the Church Fathers. I traced the doctrine of the Holy Trinity back to Athanasius, a 4th-century bishop. I quickly learned that before Athanasius there was no form of trinitarianism as we know it. A contemporary of Athanasius was another bishop called Arius who held the doctrine that the members of the Holy Trinity were not equal to, or the same as, each other. He believed that God the Father had primacy over Christ. In AD325 the Church leaders held a council, since known as the Council of Nicea. At this gathering of theologians and clergy it was decided that the Church would adopt officially the position of Athanasius over the views of Arius and that Arius's version of theology would be condemned as heretical. So, Athanasius has simply triumphed over Arius in imposing on Christianity the false doctrine of the Trinity.

And so you believe that the machinations of the early Church over this matter were really a conspiracy?

That's correct. I also assert that to fully support Athanasius, the Church elders deliberately altered the text of the Bible by modifying crucial passages. Let me give you an example. The first epistle of John, chapter 5, verse 7 says: "There are three that bear record in heaven, the Father, the Word and the Holy Ghost: and these three are one." These words did not appear in the Bible before the Council of Nicea. Clearly, the Church Fathers preferred to butcher the Scriptures rather than accept Arius.

So, put simply, what would be your position on the concept of the Holy Trinity?

Put simply? Well, it is this: only the Father is supreme. The Son is a separate being, different from the Father both in substance and in nature. Christ is not truly God, but is the so-called Word and Wisdom made flesh – divine to be sure, but only so far as divinity is communicated to the Son by the Father.

These views were dangerous, were they not?

Yes, indeed they were. Arianism had been decreed as heresy since the 4th century, and although the English government introduced modern enlightened laws during my lifetime, Arianism was still considered heretical here. In 1689 Parliament passed the Toleration Act, which offered religious freedom to all faiths with the marked exceptions of Catholicism and Arianism. Obviously, such prejudice affected me personally.

How so?

When I received my BA in 1665, I was required to attest acceptance of the Thirty-Nine Articles of the Anglican Church. This I was happy to do, because at this time I had not yet come to see the truth of Arius. Two years later, when I was awarded my Fellowship, I again agreed to swear allegiance to the Faith. Then, in 1669, I attested to the conditions of the Church for a third time. But on this occasion I was made to promise that at some point in the not-too-distant future I would take Holy Orders, because this was a condition of holding the Lucasian Professorship.

And you could not contemplate this because of your unorthodox views on the Trinity?

Precisely. I could not in all honesty swear to accept the conventional idea of the Trinity. It was Isaac Barrow who saved my career. By then he was the King's Chaplain. He managed to convince Charles to make all holders of the Lucasian Chair exempt from the requirement of taking Holy Orders.

It must have been quite an accomplishment on Barrow's part because, presumably, you could tell no one of your reasons for not wanting to take Holy Orders.

Naturally. I couldn't even tell Barrow. He acted entirely out of a desire not to lose me. If he had failed, I would have resigned my chair and the course of my career would have been very different indeed.

THE LIGHT IN THE CRUCIBLE

Although Isaac Newton was a great empirical scientist whose work was guided by mathematical rigour, he had a remarkably versatile imagination. He sincerely believed that devotion to alchemy and an investigation of arcane and mystical principles could bear valuable fruit in his quest for knowledge. Some of his associates (especially Robert Boyle) had a keen interest in the occult, but most scientists of Newton's time were either afraid to delve too deeply into natural magic or they considered the study of Hermetic knowledge and alchemy to be a waste of time and effort.

One of the things that often surprises people about your life and work is that you expended so much time in the study of alchemy, exotica and the occult. What set you off on that track?

This question of surprise is really a matter of perspective. I have always believed that a good natural philosopher, or scientist, should never turn away from any source of knowledge that will increase his understanding of the universe. In fact, I would take it further and say it is the *duty* of the scientist to seek to understand God's universe. When I was a young man I came to the conclusion that comprehending the world in which we live is possible only by studying God's "Word" *and* God's "Work". By this I mean the Holy Scriptures and Nature. Nature does not just mean what we readily observe – a study of this would get us only so far. We must delve ever deeper, and if what you call the occult is a path to that understanding, then I have no qualms about following it. I would be a coward to do otherwise, and I would not be serving Our Lord in the best way I could.

But looking back on it, do you think the great effort you put into your alchemical experiments was worthwhile?

Absolutely I do. I achieved many great things in my life, but perhaps the most important was the elucidation of the law of universal gravitation. This became the centrepiece to my *Principia Mathematica* and lies at the very heart of physics. And how do you think I arrived at this law? It was not through mathematical investigations alone, but through combining many facets of my learning. From many years of alchemical experiments, I was able to observe in the crucible forces of attraction and repulsion between small particles. I then concluded that similar (but not identical) forces might be responsible for keeping the planets in orbit.

And, of course, conducting these experiments was extremely risky, was it not?

Indeed it was, very dangerous. I don't think many people realize just how dangerous it was. Alchemy was not only illegal and punishable by death: if any of my many enemies in the academic world had gleaned the merest fraction of my work as an alchemist I would have been ruined.

But you believed in the path you were following and you risked the danger.

I had no choice. You see, I have been aware since

my earliest days as a student that I am very special. I have known almost my entire life that I was created by the Lord to serve a higher purpose. I could not turn away from this calling – that would have been the ultimate sin.

So what exactly were you trying to do?

The objective of all alchemists is to forge the Philosopher's Stone – a material which can (on the most fundamental level) turn any base metal into gold. The first thing I did was to study the great works of the alchemical tradition. I searched for sources in every possible place. From the late 1660s I travelled to Little Britain in London, where a particular supplier of arcane books, William Cooper, had a shop in which he kept many illegal and heretical texts he made available only to special customers. There I obtained such works as the *Theatrum Chemicum* by Lazarus Zetzner, works by George Ripley, translations of the magus Cornelius Agrippa, the books of the English alchemist Thomas Vaughan, and many others. After years of working through these books I began simple experiments myself, mixing reagents as recommended in the ancient texts. The most important of these texts is the *Emerald Tablet*, an ancient set of instructions that dates from the dawn of civilization.

And what sort of instructions did you follow?

At its root, alchemy is a set of elaborate laboratory procedures. I'll try to explain it step by step. First, I mixed three substances: a metal ore, usually impure iron; another metal, such as mercury; and an acid of organic origin, most typically citric acid from fruit or vegetables. These I ground together for anything up to six months, to ensure complete mixing. All the time, I heated the mixture carefully in a crucible. This was a dangerous process because toxic fumes were often produced and there was always the risk of mercury poisoning. Next, I dissolved the mixture in an acid. I evaporated and reconstituted the material using the technique of distillation. This was the most delicate and time-consuming step and I sometimes spent a year or more distilling one mixture. My laboratory furnace was never allowed to go out, and indeed there was a serious accident in my rooms in 1677 when a fire broke out. When I felt the time was right, I ended the distillation process and sealed the distillate in a special container which I warmed carefully. After cooling the material, I was able to obtain a white solid. In alchemical circles this is known as the White Stone.

Is this the Philosopher's Stone?

No, unfortunately not. The White Stone is said to be able to transmute base metals into silver, but I never continued along that path.

And you never did forge the Philosopher's Stone?

No, I did not. Early on in my quest I succeeded in creating the "Star Regulus of Mars". This antimony-based material is a wonderful crystalline substance which very few alchemists have ever managed to obtain. It is said to be the last stage en route to the Stone, but I could do nothing further with it.

And what do you conclude from this? Do you still believe in the basic tenets of alchemy, and that you failed simply because you were pursuing a false trail?

I have become disillusioned, yes. I do not believe the Philosopher's Stone exists. If I could not find it, no one could. I think it was really just a fantasy of the earliest alchemists. However, as I have said, many wonders came from my experiments and I could not have elucidated the law of universal gravitation if I had not devoted so much effort to my attempt to forge the Philosopher's Stone.

I've heard that there's a very personal aspect to alchemy, that each practitioner of the art worked in a different way and had different goals. Is that true?

It is. There is a great deal more to the art of alchemy than a set of laboratory procedures. Most alchemists seek unimaginable wealth and power. I, too, sought power, but it was of a different kind. I was trying to forge the Philosopher's Stone because I believed that with it I could unlock the secrets of the microcosmic world. I believed it held the key to understanding how the most basic elements of the material world combine and how the forces that act between these particles might behave.

One of the few close personal relationships in your life was with a young mathematician and mystic named Nicolas Fatio du Duillier. Would you agree that he had a significant influence on your thinking about the occult?

Fatio was a dear friend for a while and he was a very clever young man. Yes, he did influence my thinking. As I have said, I do have a very receptive mind and I do not fear treading paths rarely taken by others. Fatio was very knowledgeable and when I first met him he had already been interested in the occult for many years. He was not held back by the foibles of polite society nor even by orthodox moral strictures. He taught me a great deal. He was also blessed with the energy and daring of youth and he encouraged me to become even more liberated in my desire to find the ultimate answers to the deepest questions.

Did Fatio lead you into what we would call the "black arts"?

That, young man, is a matter for me, Fatio and Our Lord. I have said that I would do anything to serve God's purpose. Let us leave it at that.

THE SECRETS OF THE ANCIENTS

By the time he left Cambridge in 1696, Isaac
Newton had taken alchemy as far as he could.
But his occult interests extended far beyond
alchemy. He made an intensive study of
astrology and was fascinated by numerology.
He believed that the ancient philosophers,
the Assyrian and Babylonian mystics and the
prophets of the Old Testament all possessed
a unique wisdom that would be of enormous
value to him in his quest to unravel the secrets
of the universe. To access this knowledge he
taught himself ancient Greek and Hebrew so
that he could go back to original sources for
his research.

We've talked about your fascination with alchemy and your unorthodox approach to religion. You were also interested in the lost knowledge of the Ancients, the teachings of the Babylonians and the ancient Egyptians. What led you into this and what did you gain from it?

I was drawn to this subject when I began to question some of the accepted notions of orthodox Anglicanism. When I concluded that the official view of the Trinity was nothing more than man-made dogma, I began to question some of the other givens. I started to wonder what else had been left out of the Bible and what else had been fabricated. This led me to a deep study of ancient religions and I began to realize that the wise men of ancient times, the ancient Hebrew tribes and the Egyptians, knew far more about the universe and the way it operates than did people of my own time. In keeping with my insistence that all knowledge is valuable and that no areas should remain dark, I spent many years learning as much as possible about the ancient arts. I've described two of the things that led me to the law of universal gravitation – mathematics and alchemy. But there was a third strand: the wisdom of the Ancients.

How so?

For me, King Solomon is the ultimate Hermetic authority. I once described him as "the greatest philosopher in the world" and I have spent many thousands of hours unravelling his teachings. The focus of my attention was Old Testament descriptions of Solomon's Temple taken from the book of Ezekiel. I studied these in three different languages. The temple was originally built around 1000BC, on a site then already sacred to the Jews. Solomon's Temple was the most hallowed symbol of wisdom and faith, a place as revered as the Pyramids or Stonehenge were to different civilizations. My objective was to draw the floor-plan of the temple, because I believe that Solomon had encoded into this design the wisdom of the Ancients which lay at the heart of the Old Testament. I also reached the conclusion that by using Solomon's floor-plan as a key I could prophesy future events by analyzing the Bible. The floor-plan acted as a template because its dimensions and geometry offer clues to timescales and to the pronouncements of the great Biblical prophets, especially Ezekiel and Daniel. Combining this floor-plan with my interpretations of the Scriptures allowed me to produce an even more detailed outline for writing a chronology of both the past and the future. For example, I was able to assign dates for such events as the "Second Coming of Christ" and the "Day of Judgment".

But what does all this have to do with science?

I was coming to that. The configuration of Solomon's Temple also enabled me to develop an image of gravitation. I described the ancient temple in one of my notebooks as "a fire for offering sacrifices that burned perpetually in the middle of a sacred place", and I visualized the centre of the temple as a fire around which the believers assembled. I called this arrangement a *prytaneum*, and I quickly realized that it acted as a metaphor for the cosmos. The image of a fire at the centre of the temple with disciples arranged in a circle around the flame was another trigger in moulding my concept of universal gravitation.

But how? I don't really see the connection.

Is it not obvious? Instead of simply seeing the
rays of light radiating *outward* from the fire at the
centre of the temple, I imagined them as a force
attracting the disciples *toward* the centre. Now the
parallels between the solar system and the temple
are apparent, are they not? The disciples represent
the planets, and the temple fire, which I call "the
fire at the heart of the world", represents the Sun.
Combined with the action of forces I had observed in
the crucible and my mathematical rules, this image
gave me the idea that there was an invisible force
that acted between all objects and that its power
diminished as the objects were moved further apart.

GRAVITATION AND MOTION

Newton's work to describe the three laws of
motion was a thread in his elucidation of a
mathematical model to describe gravity. A blend
of alchemy, ancient religions and mathematics
helped him to formulate a mathematical
framework to explain the effect of gravity, but
not the mechanism of how gravity works. This
is not surprising, because even today physicists
have no definite explanation to answer the
fundamental questions: How do matter and
gravity interact in the way they do? Is there a
medium through which gravity operates? And
if there is, what is it and what is its nature?

One of the most important parts of the Principia *is your description of the three laws of motion. Can you explain these?*

The first law states that every object in a state of uniform motion will remain in that state of motion unless an external force is applied to it. In other words, all physical objects possess "inertia" or a natural tendency to move. So, to stop this motion, or to deflect an object from a straight path, one needs to apply a force. The great Galileo was the first to describe this phenomenon in scientific terms.

What did Galileo discover?

He realized the basic idea of "inertia". But he did not formulate an empirical law to describe how forces and inertia correlate.

What does the second law tell us?

This law states that if you do exert a force on
an object, it will accelerate. In other words, its
velocity will change in the direction of the force
– it accelerates in the direction in which you
push it. Furthermore, this acceleration is directly
proportional to the force you exert. For example, if
you are pushing on an object, causing it to accelerate,
and then you start to push, say, three times harder,
the acceleration will be three times greater. At the
same time, this acceleration is inversely proportional
to the mass of the object. So, if you are pushing with
equal force on two objects, and one of the objects has
twice the mass of the other, it will accelerate at one
half the value of the other.

Presumably, the calculus you developed could be used

to calculate the acceleration of the object. Can you give us a brief explanation of your calculus?

I do so hate having to explain mathematics to dunderheads who have no clue. But very well, if you want to know. There are two types of calculus, called *differentiation* and *integration*. Each of these is a method of manipulating algebraic formulae. Suppose we have a formula describing the speed of an object, say one of Galileo's cannonballs in freefall from the top of the Leaning Tower of Pisa. We can find the acceleration experienced by the object by carrying out a mathematical process on the formula called differentiation. In a similar way, if you have a formula describing the acceleration of an object, you may find its speed at any given moment by conducting another mathematical process on the formula, the reverse of differentiation, a process called integration. Differentiation of a formula takes us one way, integration takes us back again — they are really two sides of the same coin.

Your second law of motion is the most important — is that right?

Well, they are all as one to me. But the second law does offer the most important practical uses, I suppose. It describes a direct mathematical relationship between force and motion. It enables engineers to apply this mathematics to create better, more efficient machines and it helps them understand how force may be translated into motion. This is the essence of all engineering.

Yes, quite. And the third law?

For every action there is an equal and opposite reaction. This is the most easily observed. It is exactly what happens when, for example, one steps off a boat onto the river bank. As we step onto the bank, the boat moves away from us in the opposite direction.

We've talked at length about alchemy and the occult tradition, but in your published scientific work you could not even allude to these things. Could you explain how you came to distil arcane ideas into your succinct and all-embracing law of universal gravitation?

My mind kept returning to the concept of Solomon's Temple and the *prytaneum*. I also knew that inertia would mean that the Moon would move forever in a straight line unless a force was acting upon it. The Moon must be pulled toward the Earth like the disciples drawn to the flame. There must be a perfect balance – gravity and inertia cancelling out so that the Moon orbits the Earth. A good analogy for this is to imagine a stone on a string being whirled around your head. Obviously, the stone does not fall back and hit you on the head, nor does it fly off. And the longer the string, the longer the stone takes to orbit your head. This concept fascinated me and I immediately tried to formulate a law to quantify the forces at work.

And how did you do that?

Through many long hours of experiment and calculation. Eventually, I concluded that the distance between two objects and the force of gravity that keeps one of them in orbit around the other fit a strict mathematical relationship.

The inverse square law?

That's correct. I could show with great accuracy that the force of gravity decreases with distance according to this relationship. The inverse square law is a simple mathematical relationship which states that the force of gravity between two objects is proportional to the inverse square of their distance apart. So, imagine two planets A and B. If planet A orbits the Sun at a certain distance, another planet B (of equal mass) orbiting at twice the distance will experience a force of gravity one-quarter the value experienced by planet A. If another planet of equal mass, planet C, orbits at a distance three times greater than A, it will experience a force of gravity only one-ninth that experienced by planet A.

There was one particular piece of research that led the way. The Moon orbits the Earth, and, of course, neither the size of the Moon nor the size of the Earth changes. Also, their distance apart stays about the same, and the Moon's orbit is close to a circle. Now, I knew accurately the time it takes the Moon to make one orbit of the Earth, and this does not deviate either. I called the force that counterbalances inertia and keeps the Moon in orbit "gravity". This force determines the time it takes for the Moon to orbit the Earth. So, knowing this time period, I could use the inverse square law to work out the strength of the Earth's gravitational pull at the distance of the Moon.

This works perfectly for a simple two-body system, far from the influence of any other matter. But surely the planets in the solar system all influence each other?

Well yes, to a certain degree. Take the example of planet A orbiting the Sun. If the second planet B is a long way from A, and farther from the Sun than planet

A, it will have some effect on the orbit of A about the Sun, but its effect will diminish greatly with distance. This phenomenon is known as "orbital perturbation", and to obtain a very accurate description of the orbit of A about the Sun, this effect created by B must be taken into account. This puzzle is known as a three-bodied problem and there is no known mathematical method for solving it. Obviously, if there are more planets in the vicinity of planet A and the Sun, the problem becomes even more complicated and impossible to describe perfectly.

So, to go back to the order in which you developed the law of universal gravitation. First, a collection of influences led you to the concept of a force to counterbalance inertia. Then you were able to demonstrate that this force perfectly fitted the inverse square law. The next step would have been to try to explain how this force operates.

Yes, it would have been, but this work brought me no closer to understanding how gravity works. What is the medium through which this force operates? How can two objects that are a certain distance apart affect one another at all? I came to the conclusion that the force that holds planets in their orbits is related to the forces at work in the crucible attracting and repelling small particles of matter. I also knew that there are forces in Nature that hold some sorts of metal together when they are put in close proximity, and there is also a force of attraction that brings little pieces of paper to an amber rod that has been rubbed with fur. I have done these experiments and I have seen these forces at work, just as I see the Moon orbit the Earth.

So, you're saying that there's really only one force at work in Nature?

No, that's not what I'm saying at all. I believe that there are several different types of force, but that they are interrelated and all operate through a common medium.

Did you reach any conclusions about the nature of this medium?

Yes, I did. Gravity, I realized, is a universal force. There is some underlying way in which forces can act over empty space. I believe these forces act through the spirit of Jesus Christ. God is one, *not three*. He is not outside the universe, but a part of it, a unifier. However, by what means does he keep the planets in motion and particles moving? He uses gravity and these other mysterious forces. But how? I questioned this for a long time. I implored God to tell me. And then, in a flash, in a moment of divine inspiration, it came to me. God uses the body, the essence, the spirit of Christ as the medium for these forces. God's son became incarnate once before, but he is immortal, pure spirit, and he can take on any form. He can guide the atoms of the universe. He may steer the planets in their paths and make suns burn with furious flame. I could never publish this hypothesis, of course, but it is the best explanation I have.

It's a very radical notion and impossible to prove, I assume?

I imagine many people would consider it radical. And no, of course, it cannot be proven. But then no physicist can *prove* their own hypotheses on this matter, can they? If one day a better explanation is arrived at I will, of course, give it my due attention. Until then my hypothesis satisfies me.

ON THE NATURE OF LIGHT

In some of his earliest studies Newton
investigated the properties of light. To help
with his experiments and observations he
created practical tools, such as his excellent
reflecting telescope. He applied the same
mathematical rigour he used to explain the
forces governing motion and gravity to
describe the true nature and behaviour of
light. From this work he was able to discover
a set of universal laws which he described in
great detail in his second masterwork, *Opticks*,
which was published in 1704.

When did you first become interested in the study of light?

My interest was first piqued while reading Descartes's theories on the nature of light in the books owned by Mr Clark, the apothecary. Descartes believed that light was a "pressure" transmitted through a transparent medium he called "the ether". Sight, he believed, was due to this pressure impinging on the optic nerve. He also thought that colour was produced by packets of light in the form of rotating spheres. Of course, when I first read these things I had no idea whether or not such hypotheses were true. Descartes was a great thinker but he performed few experiments, and I know his theories on the nature of light and the way it is transmitted could not have been derived from these experiments. So for me, they were far from empirical enough.

*So, what was the prevailing theory of light in the 1660s
and 1670s? Was Descartes's view the accepted wisdom?*

There were at least two different models. Some
experimenters believed light was wavelike, like a
vibrating string of a violin or a taut rope that has been
flicked. Others held the view that light was made up
of parcels or packets that were somehow transmitted
through space. I was more inclined to the former
description, but I was never able to prove this correct.

*Well, that isn't really surprising, because even in
my day, in the early 21st century, scientists are still
uncertain about the answer to this question. So when
did you start to experiment with light yourself?*

Experiments with light were the very first researches
I conducted – soon after I had settled in Cambridge.

In 1664 I acquired a prism at a country fair held in Stourbridge near Cambridge. I bought it for a few pennies from a stall selling quack elixirs and novelties. I began experimenting with it straightaway. The Ancients knew that a prism could produce a spectrum of colours ranging from red light to blue. I realized quickly that "normal" light is best described as white light and is split by the prism into its constituent parts. Furthermore, this happens because the prism refracts the light and bends blue light more than red, so that it produces a spectrum of colours.

And you were able to prove this?

Yes. I split the light with a prism, then I blocked off most of the emergent light with a sheet of paper, allowing just one colour through. I found that red was the least refracted observable colour and violet the most. This has become known as the *experimentum cruces*.

But you didn't stop there?

No, I created another experiment in which I split light with a prism, then passed this light through a lens which focused the emergent beam onto a wall. When this happened, a white spot was produced at the target. Finally, I repeated this experiment but with a cogged wheel placed after the lens. With this wheel I was able to block out one colour coming from the lens before it was focused to a point on the wall. I found that if I blocked a colour, a coloured rather than a white spot was produced. The colour of the spot depended upon which colour I removed from the spectrum emerging from the lens.

And am I right in saying that you put yourself at some risk with a few of the experiments you conducted in those early days?

I think now that I may have been a little foolhardy. I nearly blinded myself and could not see properly for days after I stared at the Sun for too long trying to discern coloured rings caused by the glare. But perhaps the most dangerous thing I did was an experiment to see how the curvature of the eye affected the appearance of an object. I placed the tip of a fine dagger between the back of my eyeball and the bone of my eye socket and moved it around. This altered the shape of my eye, and as a result, I observed several strange coloured circles.

But you decided not to publish your discoveries at this time?

No, of course I didn't publish them. I was a young student, barely a BA. I kept my observations to myself recorded in notebooks and I expanded on these over the years. They acted as the basic framework for my book *Opticks*. The Dutch scientist, Christiaan Huygens, elaborated on some of my early ideas which had appeared in brief papers through the Royal Society long before *Opticks* was published. His own book, *Traité de la lumière*, bore many of the hallmarks of my work from a decade earlier.

I can understand why you wouldn't have published before you'd established yourself, but by the mid-1670s you were a respected scientist. Why did you wait another 30 years before publishing Opticks?

I had written the bulk of this book during the 1670s, but I could not bring myself to offer it to the Royal

Society. I did not trust them, especially Hooke. I waited until I felt the time was right for the Royal Society to do justice to my work – this was after Hooke was in his grave. In retrospect, I regret that my prevarication delayed publication by almost three decades, but I was not to blame.

MAKING A QUALITY TELESCOPE

From his earliest days at Cambridge, Newton
was dedicated to astronomy. But, at the same
time, he was frustrated by the poor quality of
telescopes he could obtain. Never being a man
to accept what was handed down to him if he
believed he could do better, during the late
1660s he began to produce his own lenses and
to improve the refracting telescopes available
to him. However, he soon found that the
performance of these devices could be improved
only so far, and this pushed him into making
his own high-quality optical instruments and
creating a practical reflecting telescope.

When did you first become interested in astronomy?

Again, it was thanks to the library in the Clark's house. There was a copy of *Starry Messenger*, which Galileo wrote soon after he had perfected the telescope in 1609. Galileo produced exquisite drawings of the Moon in which he detailed craters and mountains, ravines and canyons. He turned his telescope toward Jupiter and became the first to observe its moons. This book more than any others I read in that library inspired me to imagine conducting my own experiments.

But you were shocked by the inadequacy of telescopes that you had access to.

Yes, I certainly was. Galileo had produced the finest instruments of his day with magnifying powers of

30 or 40, but the field of view was narrow and they had a lot of what astronomers call "chromatic aberration". This is caused by imperfections in the lenses and it means that rays of different wavelength are not brought together at the same focal point and so they produce a distorted image. I decided to take an entirely different approach. Galileo's telescopes were all based on the design of the original inventor, the Dutchman, Hans Lippershey. They were what are called "refracting telescopes". This type of telescope uses two lenses positioned at each end of a tube to produce a magnified image. An alternative device, called a "reflecting telescope", uses one lens and a mirror to create an image. This had been suggested in Galileo's day, and one had actually been built by a mathematician named James Gregory, but the image it produced was almost useless.

*But you succeeded where Gregory had failed. And is it
true that you made all the components yourself?*

Yes, I succeeded in making a practical reflecting
telescope, and yes I did make all the parts of the
telescope myself. I tried to get a perfect mirror
and exquisitely ground lenses made by specialist
craftsmen in London, but they could not do it. I was
forced to grind my own lens and to make my own
tubes and mountings. I must admit, the end result
was a beautiful thing. Reflecting telescopes can be
made much smaller than refracting telescopes, which
require the lenses to be placed far apart along the
tube. My telescope was no more than six inches long
and mounted on a tiny stand. With it, I was able to
obtain a clear image at a magnification of 40.

And this led to your first introduction to the scientific

community beyond Cambridge, did it not?

Yes. Isaac Barrow was greatly taken with my telescope, and in 1671 he arranged for it to be demonstrated before a meeting of the Royal Society. The astronomer John Flamsteed was very impressed, as were Christopher Wren and the Secretary of the Royal Society, Henry Oldenburg. They even arranged a demonstration of my device for the king, Charles II, who was apparently greatly excited by it. Within a few weeks I had been invited to become a Fellow of the Royal Society.

A FRESH START

The 1690s marked a time of great change in Newton's life. Since arriving in Cambridge in 1661 he had led the life of a cloistered academic, rarely involving himself in the world beyond the walls of Trinity College. In 1687 his greatest work, *Principia Mathematica*, was published, and consequently he was considered the most important scientist in the world. But then Newton's life changed dramatically. In 1693 he experienced what may have been a nervous breakdown, and ceased to be involved in practical scientific experiments. Then in 1696 he moved to London where he took up an administrative post as Warden of the Royal Mint.

Would it be fair to say that sometime during the 1690s
you began to lose interest in science?

No, that is by no means true. I have never lost
interest in science.

But in 1696 you left Cambridge University and moved
to London. You did very little science after that.

But *Opticks* was published eight years after I left
Cambridge and I remained president of the Royal
Society, did I not? It was not science I grew weary of
– science is an endless mystery and a never-ending
inspiration to me. What is true is that, from the early
1690s, I became less interested in experiment.

Do you feel this is because you reached a point where you
could go no further?

I think that is right, yes. With both my pure science experiments and my alchemical work I took things as far as I could go. I hit a wall, if you like. The material in my *Opticks* was based on work completed between the 1660s and 1690s. I continued to be interested in science and to guide its progress through the Royal Society, of which I was a very active and energetic president for 23 years. But leaving Cambridge was a declaration of intent. I had exhausted the possibilities of experiment and research and wanted to do something entirely different.

This must have been very difficult for you. Indeed, it has been said that around this time you suffered a temporary mental collapse. Do you feel you can talk about this?

Yes, I'm aware of these stories, and the fact is, no one but I knows what this episode entailed, and even I have only a distorted memory of it. I think too much has been made of it. Apparently, I wrote a couple of strange letters to colleagues and a couple of visitors to Cambridge reported that I was in an especially uncommunicative state of mind.

All this was when?

1693.

This was also soon after you parted company with Nicolas Fatio du Duillier and about the time you stopped your alchemical studies. Is there any connection between these things?

As I explained earlier, for me knowledge is all-embracing. I don't compartmentalize learning. So, alchemy, the Hermetic tradition, ancient religions and science all meld together. I have always tried to find answers to the greatest mysteries, and these studies were my tools. By the 1690s, I had been using those tools for some three decades and I was, well, very tired. People have tried to explain my strange mood in 1693 as the result of inhaling too many noxious gases in my laboratory, or perhaps the result of mercury poisoning. Others have tried to suggest that my so-called nervous breakdown came as a result of delving too deeply into the occult. I'm afraid the real reason is altogether more prosaic. I was worn out. I had gone as far as I could with the resources available to me, and I needed a fresh start.

And that came in the form of a position at the Royal Mint in London?

Yes. I saw it as an exciting adventure, a challenge.

I moved to the capital and I became an administrator. I have always been interested in organization. That has been one of my strengths as a scientist: I always recorded my discoveries with great clarity and method. This is also what is required of any good administrator. As well as this, I was excited by the prospect of being at the centre of such an important institution as the Royal Mint, at the very heart of the financial world.

It was also, of course, a job made for a scientist because there were technical aspects to the position where a knowledge of chemistry was an important bonus.

Absolutely. I was initially offered the position of Warden of the Mint, and then in 1700 I became Master of the Mint. I was most attracted to the task because I was required to use my scientific knowledge in making the minting process as efficient as possible. Indeed, I succeeded in streamlining the production of coin metal at the mint.

I understand you were merciless when it came to "clippers" who snipped off and sold bits of gold and silver coins?

Clippers are common thieves. They are no better than those who rob the innocent or steal from homes. Actually, their crimes are even worse because they are crimes against the state, and their actions threaten to undermine the status quo. I view clippers as traitors. And yes, before you ask, I did indeed attend every hanging of a clipper, even though I did not need to do so. I am proud of this. I also hunted down suspects with great fervour. As far as I am aware, none escaped my net.

*There was one particular villain you pursued and did
actually bring to trial for treason, wasn't there?*

You are referring to William Chaloner. Some people
have viewed the man as a romantic figure, a heroic
anti-Establishment daredevil, if you will, but he was
actually a traitor, and he met a traitor's end.

*You insisted he face a charge of treason and you ignored
all pleas for clemency.*

Yes, I did. His trial took place a little over a year
after I started at the Mint, and I wanted to set an
example. Chaloner was not some petty thief, he
was a brazen forger and counterfeiter. He faced the
ultimate punishment. He was dragged on a sledge
to Tyburn gallows where he was hanged until almost
unconscious, disembowelled, then quartered.

Do you not feel your actions were unnecessarily ruthless, even inhumane?

Not in the slightest. Indeed, I find this a strange question. Any of my contemporaries would have done precisely the same thing. Criminals cannot be allowed to get away with their crimes, and those who flout the law must be made examples of.

LONDON LIFE

Newton's character had always been a strange
amalgam of the hermit and the social climber.
His childhood spent in Grantham, then a rather
small, sleepy town, made him curious about
the big city, but at the same time he guarded
his privacy with unusual vigour. He was an
introverted man, but he aspired to achieve
recognition beyond the academic world, and so
craved the attention of Establishment figures.
His position at the Royal Mint set him up
perfectly to fulfil this desire, and Newton seized
with both hands the opportunity it offered. His
beautiful niece stayed at his London house and
became socially advantageous to him.

*Was it difficult adjusting to your new life in London
after leaving Cambridge?*

Yes and no. Throughout my final decade in
Cambridge I spent more and more time in
the capital. Toward the end of the 1680s I had
represented the University of Cambridge as a
Member of Parliament, and this was an incredibly
eventful period in British history. William of Orange
took over the monarchy in a bloodless coup, the
Glorious Revolution of 1688. I was involved in that
process, along with my parliamentary colleagues, in
what was called the Convention Parliament. I visited
London frequently, from as early as the 1660s. I
used to catch the stagecoach from The Rose public
house in Cambridge to The Swan tavern in Gray's
Inn Lane in the heart of London. The journey was
long and uncomfortable. I purchased much of my

library in a district called Little Britain and it was here I found chemicals and alchemical apparatus. It was also in London that I bought the equipment I needed to produce my telescopes and other optical equipment. Sometimes I stayed for a few weeks. Even so, it took me a while to get used to the change in my lifestyle. In Cambridge I had a very comfortable set of rooms and my laboratory had served me well – it had evolved considerably over the decades I spent in experiment. However, Cambridge is a small town and the university is very self-contained. I had little to do with the other Fellows, and I shunned almost all social activities linked to my college.

And in London you lived the life of a socialite?

I gradually took on something of that role, yes. I wouldn't exactly describe myself as a "socialite", but

I did entertain in my house in fashionable Jermyn Street, and I did make many new acquaintances as well as professional contacts. And then, of course, there was my work, which involved managing my staff and dealing with my superiors. From 1703 I was also responsible for presiding over the Royal Society. So, all in all, I was very busy and my work was very different to the purely cerebral activities I had enjoyed as an academic.

In 1696 your niece Catherine Barton moved into your house in London. That must have presented you with another dramatic change.

Yes, of course it did, but I think it was a very successful arrangement for both of us. Catherine is a charming and intelligent girl. We got on very well. Catherine's mother was my half-sister, Hannah,

a child of my mother's second marriage to the
Reverend Barnabas Smith. Hannah had been left
destitute by the sudden death of her husband, Robert
Barton, and when Catherine was seventeen it was
decided by the family that she should be introduced
to London society. I owned a large house, and so I was
happy to have the girl in residence.

She was also a great beauty.

Indeed, and I will not deny that she was a great asset
to me. Many important figures were besotted with
Catherine, including Pierre Rémond de Montmort,
a married French bureaucrat who fell in love with her
the moment he laid eyes on her at a dinner party at
my home.

It's said that Jonathan Swift was also a suitor.

No, Swift was never a suitor, but he adored Catherine and they were close friends.

And what of Charles Montagu, Earl of Halifax, who was Chancellor of the Exchequer and close to King William?

Yes, Charles was deeply in love with Catherine. He was a man for whom I had the greatest respect, and I was very happy for this relationship to blossom. Charles was considerably older than Catherine but they were a perfect match: he was a widower and one of the richest men in Britain, with impeccable connections. Sadly, he died young, in 1715.

Surely they could never have married, though?

No, of course not. Although Catherine was my niece and Charles and I were good friends, she was nevertheless a simple country girl from the lower gentry. Montagu loved Catherine, of that there can be no doubt. In his will he left her 5,000 pounds and the wardship of his estate at Bushy Park, along with a large house in Surrey.

And within a few years Catherine married.

Yes, she married a fine man, John Conduitt, a scholar and a wealthy gentleman who became an MP. And later, when I retired from the Mint, he took over my old position as Master.

THE ROYAL SOCIETY

As a young professor, Newton had a fragile relationship with the Royal Society. This was principally because he clashed terribly with some of the key members, especially the Curator of Experiments, Robert Hooke. This conflict developed into a feud that caused Newton to shun the Society for many years. When he eventually became the President of the Royal Society a few months after Hooke died in March 1703, Newton had all portraits of his rival removed and destroyed. Afterwards, Newton became an integral part of the Royal Society and did much to improve its status and position.

Sir Isaac, do you consider your involvement with the Royal Society to have been a significant aspect of your life and career?

Indeed I do. In the early days, I was frozen out of the Society by Hooke. As I explained earlier, he did much to try to damage my reputation. As a reaction to this I came close to giving up my Fellowship. But in the end I merely kept myself to myself in Cambridge. Hooke was a bad apple, but there were many fine men at the Royal Society whom I admired. Christopher Wren was an outstanding intellect and a good man. I also considered Edmund Halley to be a remarkable talent. Both men always made me welcome, and they supported me when I took the reins at the Society in 1703.

How do you see the role of the Royal Society in your time?

Has its existence been at all relevant to the advancement of science?

Well, of course it has! The Royal Society is an immensely important institution and I can confidently take some significant credit for elevating it from a serious but rather ineffectual gathering of intellectuals to its current position as the most influential and respected academic society in the world. In the beginning, the Royal Society was little more than an informal club founded by Henry Oldenburg, Robert Boyle and Seth Ward in Oxford. Even when I was invited to become a Fellow early in 1672, the Society consisted of only a few dozen members. For many years the continued existence of the Royal Society was constantly under threat. A suitable permanent home could never be found, its finances were in a mess and it came perilously close to dissolving. Henry Oldenburg was one of the great administrators of the Society and he did an enormous amount to steer it into clearer waters. But, I have to say, it was not until I became president that the Society was truly rescued.

You were responsible for significant reforms?

Yes, I was. To begin with, I made it a priority to find a home for the Society. This I did in 1710, when we purchased a wonderful property in Crane Court, London.

And what of the science? Can you explain how the Royal Society affected the progress of science?

I placed great emphasis on making the Society run properly because I believed that this was essential if it were to play its role in moving science forward. And, of course, it is the advancement of science that is the real *raison d'être* of the Society. The Royal Society promotes this in many ways. First, it acts as a meeting place for the greatest minds of the age – not just pure scientists but also men such as Samuel Pepys or Wren, polymathic figures with a keen interest in science. The simple act of meeting, talking and lecturing is crucial. Second, there are also the many experiments funded and organized by the Society. Most of these are conducted far from the spotlight, while others are demonstrations for all members to witness. Finally, there are the publications financed by the Royal Society. We have a journal, *Philosophical Transactions*. This was the first scientific journal ever created and its value is hard to overestimate. It produced the template for all scientific publishing and offered a unique system for the researcher. A Fellow could write about a piece of research he had conducted and publish it for the other members to study and comment upon. This created a healthy and progressive forum for intellectual advance. But the *Transactions* are not the only form of communication the Royal Society provided. It has financed the publication of many important books, including my own *Principia Mathematica* and *Opticks*.

And Robert Hooke's Micrographia, *of course.*

Yes, that too.

A REMARKABLE LEGACY

The work of Isaac Newton was truly revolutionary, sparking a transformative movement, which began in England some 60 years after his death before spreading across the world – the Industrial Revolution. This was a paradigm shift in the history of civilization, taking humankind from a state in which the main focus was agriculture and small-scale crafts to one in which industry, mechanization and technology became paramount. Newton's experimental work and theories took science from being an almost exclusively cerebral activity and turned it into something practical, a discipline which increasingly benefits us all.

*Some men wish to be remembered as "good", others
as people who have changed the world. Few can claim
to have been both. How would you most like to be
remembered?*

I believe I have led a good life. I have been honest
to my conscience, I have been honest to my Lord. I
have devoted myself to the noblest causes, and I have
achieved great things. I would rather be remembered
as a man who made a difference. *I* know whether or
not I have led a Christian life, and so does God. I care
little for what other people may think about that.

What would you say was your greatest achievement?

I find it hard to differentiate between aspects of
my work. To me it's all one. My journey from the
cradle has been one in which first I learned from my

antecedents, then I tried to emulate them, and finally I surpassed them. I cannot say that my work in optics is any more or any less worthy than what I discovered about gravity or the behaviour of objects in motion. Is my discovery of a practical form of calculus any more or any less significant than my telescope? I cannot say. Humanity being what it is, I imagine I will be remembered for the most trivial aspects of my work.

I sense you are very keen to preserve your reputation as an empirical scientist. I noticed in your answer that you didn't mention alchemy or your researches into the nature of ancient religions or mysticism.

I have had to be secretive about these things all my life, and defensiveness is ingrained in me. I have instructed my closest friends and my – shall we call them "disciples"? – to destroy a large body of my work on alchemy and not to speak of my involvement in the arcane, even after my death. I have devoted my life to the search for knowledge, and I have absolutely no shame concerning the methods I employed. But I know the vindictiveness of people, and I know how my many detractors would love nothing better than to use my fascination with unorthodox subjects to damage my legacy.

It seems to me that the greatest achievement for anyone is to do something which will benefit future generations, so that they are remembered and celebrated for what they have left the world. Do you imagine others taking your lead and using your discoveries for the benefit of humanity?

This is now my most fervent wish, but it was not always so. When I was young I sought knowledge for its own sake. I was perhaps more arrogant. As I have grown older, it has become more important to me that I be remembered for my work and that my achievements be used to improve the lot of mankind. I believe they will.

I have a feeling you're right, Sir Isaac. Now, could you indulge me in one last question you may find trivial, but it's one I've always wanted to ask you. Is the apple story true?

Ah yes, I'm surprised you didn't get to that one earlier. Is the apple story true? Well, I'm sorry, young man, I'm afraid I'm going to have to disappoint you … and leave you wondering!

REFILL?

For information about Isaac Newton on the web, the best starting point is the Isaac Newton Institute for Mathematical Sciences at: http://www.newton.cam.ac.uk/newton.html

BOOKS ABOUT ISAAC NEWTON

Richard Westfall, *Never At Rest: A Biography of Isaac Newton* (Cambridge: Cambridge University Press, 1980; New York: Barnes & Noble, 1983)

Michael White, *Isaac Newton: The Last Sorcerer* (London: 4th Estate, 1997; New York: Helix Books, 1999)

BOOKS ABOUT THE HISTORY OF SCIENCE

Daniel J. Boorstin, *The Discoverers* (London: Phoenix Press, Orion, 1983; New York: Random House, 1983)

Melvyn Bragg, *On Giant's Shoulders* (London: Hodder and Stoughton, 1998; New York: Wiley, 2000)

Jacob Bronowski, *The Ascent of Man* (London: BBC Books, 1973; Boston: Little, Brown & Co., 1973)

Arthur Koestler, *The Sleepwalkers* (London: Penguin, 1964; New York: Arkana, 1990)

BOOKS ABOUT THE ROYAL SOCIETY

John Gribbin, *Fellowship* (London: Penguin, 2005; New York: Penguin 2006)

INDEX